D1609081

JOLLY
JELLYFISH

by
Mignonne Gunasekara

BEARPORT
PUBLISHING

Minneapolis, Minnesota

PHOTO CREDITS

All images are courtesy of Shutterstock.com, unless otherwise specified. With thanks to Getty Images, Thinkstock Photo and iStockphoto. Plant Vectors Throughout – Baksiabat, MicroOne. Front Cover – Astridlike, Andrea Izzotti, GParker, karnizz, Malgorzata Litkowsk. 4–5 – Rich Carey. 6–7 – Mark William Kirkland, divedog, Martin Prochazkacz. 8–9 – Vojce, Alexey Masliy, John_Walker, Love the wind. 10–11 – Becky Gill, Alex Staroseltsev, Damsea, Imagine Earth Photography. 12–13 – John Wollwerth, Kateryna Mostova, divedog. 14–15 – SHIN-db, wv, Beautiful landscape, Ken Wolter. 16–17 – aaltair, Bill Roque, divedog. 18–19 – Fon Duangkamon, divedog. 20–21 – Rebecca Schreiner, zaferkizilkaya, divedog. 22–23 – NAPAPORN NONTH, Mariusz Hajdarowicz, Rich Carey.

Library of Congress Cataloging-in-Publication Data is available at www.loc.gov or upon request from the publisher.

ISBN: 978-1-64747-405-8 (hardcover)
ISBN: 978-1-64747-412-6 (paperback)
ISBN: 978-1-64747-419-5 (ebook)

© 2021 Booklife Publishing
This edition is published by arrangement with Booklife Publishing.

For more information, write to Bearport Publishing, 5357 Penn Avenue South, Minneapolis, MN 55419.
Printed in the United States of America.

CONTENTS

WELCOME TO THE AQUARIUM!

Welcome to the aquarium. Aquariums look after sea animals. Many aquariums do lots of work to protect wild animals, too.

Let's look at jellyfish. Jellyfish don't have bones, brains, or hearts. They are mostly made of water!

Let's look at eight kinds of jellyfish.

5

LION'S MANE JELLYFISH

Lion's mane jellyfish eat small fish and other jellyfish.

Tentacles

Lion's mane jellyfish live in colder waters. They have stinging tentacles that they use to catch **prey**.

Lion's mane jellyfish tentacles remind people of a lion's mane.

These tentacles can sting even after the jellyfish dies.

The lion's mane jellyfish is the largest jellyfish on Earth. Its tentacles can grow to over 10 feet (3 m) long.

FRIED EGG JELLYFISH

Can you guess how these jellyfish got their name?

Fried egg

Fried egg jellyfish look just like fried eggs moving through the water!

It normally takes two animals to make a baby. But a fried egg jellyfish can make a baby on its own.

Fried egg jellyfish eat tiny animals that float in the water.

COMPASS JELLYFISH

Bell

The top of a jellyfish body is called the **bell**.

Compass

It's easy to spot a compass jellyfish because of its **markings**. Brown lines on its bell make it look like a compass.

A compass jellyfish has 24 long, thin tentacles. It also has four mouth arms.

Mouth arms move prey to the jellyfish's mouth.

Mouth arms

CANNONBALL JELLYFISH

A cannonball jellyfish's sting is too weak to hurt humans.

Cannonball jellyfish don't have tentacles. They only have mouth arms.

Cannonball jellyfish have a special way of fighting **predators**. When they are scared, they can make **mucus**.

The mucus is **toxic**. It hurts predators and scares them away.

Some people eat cannonball jellyfish.

PACIFIC SEA NETTLE

Pacific sea nettle stings can hurt people but don't normally kill them.

A Pacific sea nettle has long tentacles and frilly mouth arms.

14

Pacific sea nettles eat fish, snails, and other jellyfish.

Pacific sea nettles can't see, but they can tell the difference between light and dark.

Prey gets stuck to a Pacific sea nettle's stinging tentacles. Then, the prey is moved to the jellyfish's mouth.

15

MOON JELLYFISH

Moon jellyfish can be found in waters around the world.

The moon jellyfish's tentacles are quite short. They are also so thin that they look like hairs.

16

Moon jellyfish can change color based on the kind of food they eat. If they eat shrimp, they can turn pink.

Moon jellyfish bells can be up to 15 inches (38 cm) wide.

The stinging parts of the moon jellyfish don't usually hurt humans.

17

SEA WASP

Sea wasp tentacles can grow up to 10 feet (3 m) long.

Sea wasps belong to a group of jellyfish called box jellyfish. This is because their bells are box-shaped.

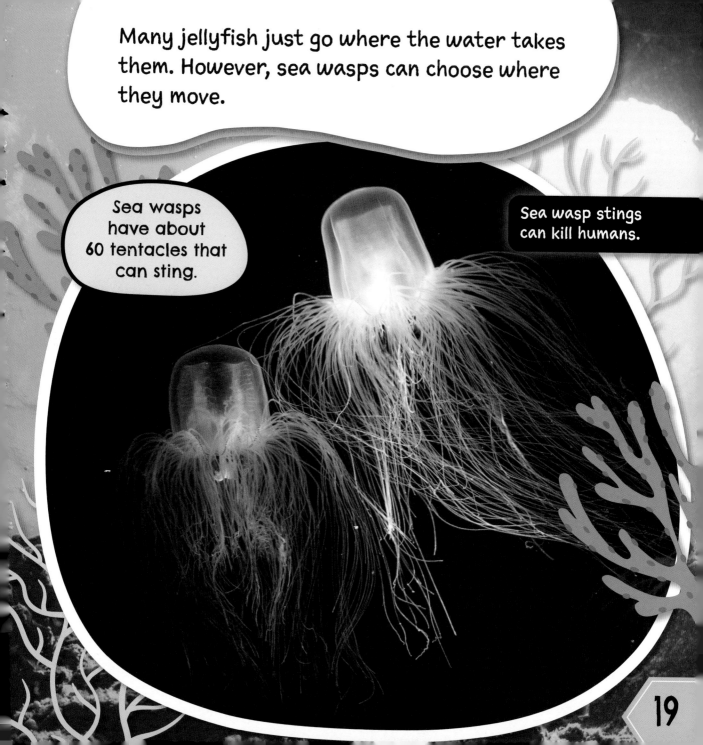

Many jellyfish just go where the water takes them. However, sea wasps can choose where they move.

Sea wasps have about 60 tentacles that can sting.

Sea wasp stings can kill humans.

19

IMMORTAL JELLYFISH

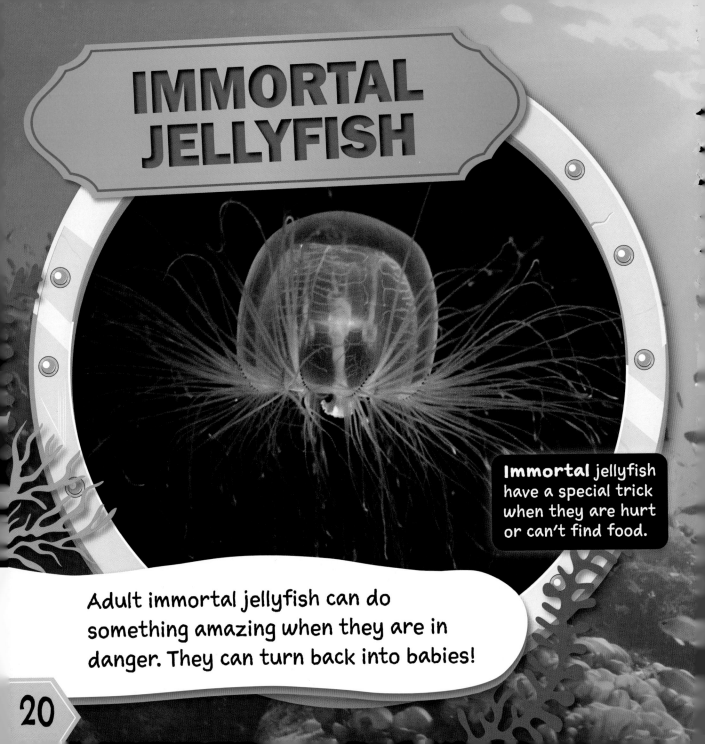

Immortal jellyfish have a special trick when they are hurt or can't find food.

Adult immortal jellyfish can do something amazing when they are in danger. They can turn back into babies!

Immortal jellyfish have been found all over the world. People think that they sometimes move along with ships.

Immortal jellyfish are only about as wide as the nail on your little finger!

THANKS FOR VISITING!

Thank you for stopping by the aquarium! If you like jolly jellyfish, there are things you can do to keep them safe.

Watch out for jellyfish on the beach!

Remember, jellyfish stings can be painful. If you see a jellyfish, don't touch it.

Throw away your trash and **recycle** what you can. This helps keep the oceans clean!

Stop garbage from ending up in the oceans that jellyfish call home.

GLOSSARY

bell the top part of a jellyfish's body

immortal living or lasting forever

markings marks or patterns on an animal

mucus a slimy substance that helps to protect and lubricate certain parts of the body

predators animals that hunt other animals for food

prey animals that are hunted by other animals for food

recycle to turn something used and unwanted into something new

toxic harmful or deadly

INDEX

24